Natalie

and the One-of-a-Kind Wonderful Day!

Other titles in the That's Nat Series

Natalie

and the One-of-a-Kind Wonderful Day!

Dandi Daley Mackall

ZONDERVAN.com/
AUTHORTRACKER
follow your favorite authors

We want to hear from you. Please send your comments about this book
to us in care of zreview@zondervan.com.

To our own "Only Katy"

ZONDERKIDZ

Natalie and the One-of-a-Kind Wonderful Day!
Copyright © 2009 by Dandi Daley Mackall
Illustrations © 2009 by Lys Blakeslee

Requests for information should be addressed to:

Zonderkidz, *Grand Rapids, Michigan* 49530

Library of Congress Cataloging-in-Publication Data

Mackall, Dandi Daley.
  Natalie and the one-of-a-kind wonderful day! / by Dandi Daley Mackall.
    p. cm. — (That's Nat! ; bk. 1)
  Summary: Five-year-old Natalie is determined to create a one-of-a-kind wonderful surprise
for her parents, but even when the results are a series of foiled attempts and ensuing
disasters, she discovers something amazing.
  ISBN 9780310715665 (softcover)
[1. Surprise — Fiction. 2. Imagination — Fiction. 3. Christian life — Fiction.] I. Title.
PZ7.M1905Nao 2009
[Fic] — dc22   2008048360

Editor: Betsy Flikkema
Art direction and design: Merit Kathan

Printed in the United States of America

13 14 15 /DCI/ 15 14 13 12 11

Table of Contents

Introducing Nat ... Pleased to Meet You

Pleased to Meet You

This is my first ever book about me. So you probably don't even know who I am. And that's okay on account of I'm going to tell you.

My name is Natalie 24. That's what.

I have other names to go with those, but I'll bet you're still stuck wondering about the 24 in my name.

"*24* isn't a name!" you say. And maybe you laugh just a little bit. "24 is a number."

That's a true thing. 24 *is* a number. It's my favorite and best number. And that's why I have it as part of my name. Get it?

So go ahead and call me Natalie 24 if you want to. I look just like somebody named 24.

And I've got PJs to prove it. My dad got me PJs that look like baseball players wore them, only littler. And that number on the back of those PJs is — you guessed it — 24, which was some great big baseball player's famous number before I took it over.

There are many more great things about 24. For one of those great things, I have a cat that goes by the name of "Percy 24."

And another great thing is that there are 24 bottles of that water that comes in bottles and is so much more fun to drink than regular water you have to catch in a glass.

Plus, there are 24 colors in a box of 24 colors.

And 24 candy bars in a box of 24 candy bars.

And 24 kindergarteners in a box of 24 kindergarteners.

And 24 cats in a box of 24 cats.

(But I made up the ones about candy bars and kindergartners and cats. And I laughed just a little bit when I told you that, which makes us even Steven on the laughing.)

So that's it. That's why my name is Natalie 24.

But here's the thing. My really good friends call me "Nat 24" or "Nat." So if you stick it out reading this book, then I guess that might could make us really good friends.

So ... I'm Nat. Pleased to meet you.

Chapter 1

Omel-Nats

Today is the day!

I am sitting up in my bed and waking all the way up. I look out my bedroom window and see dark out there, with only a little sun down low.

"Wake up, Percy 24!" I tell my sleepy cat.

"No," Percy says. He does not say no with words. He more like growls, which is cat talk for no.

"You have to get up, Percy!" I whisper-shout.

"Today, I am going to do a one-of-a-kind wonderful thing!"

Percy and I get out of bed and tippytoe to the kitchen. Why? I'll tell you why. If you *clump, clump* around here when people are still sleeping, you can get in a whole lot of trouble. That's what.

"Don't wake up Mommy," I warn Percy. "She will only want to help me make this breakfast. But I'm big enough to help myself. Plus, if Mommy helps, it won't be a wonderful surprise."

Percy tippytoes better than me. He goes right straight for his Percy dish. But there's not any Percy food in there.

"Don't worry," I whisper to Percy. "I will make

one-of-a-kind wonderful omel-nats for everybody!"

Sometimes when I stay at Granny's, she makes me omelets with eggs and cheese. She calls them mommy-lets, and we laugh our heads off. And that's how I got that idea about the omel-nats. That word sounds like omelet and Nat. See that?

Only I will make PURPLE omel-nats. I love that purple color.

I dig into Mommy's bowl place in the down low cabinet. There are little, middle, and big huge bowls down there. I don't know which bowl is the best. So I bring out all of those bowls to pick from.

Next, I open the fridge. The light is on in there. And I wonder what all the foods think about having that light on all the time when they're trying to get some sleep.

The big fat jug of milk is too big to be carried out. So I choose the little box of thick milk my dad puts into his coffee. And that works.

There's lots of other stuff in this fridge. Like orange juice. I love that orange stuff — only not when it's got pieces of itself floating around in it. I carry the juice out of the fridge and put it on the floor with Daddy's thick milk box and all the bowls.

Back in the fridge, I discover that we have a gazillion eggs. And that is a good thing I didn't even think about before. "You *have* to have eggs for omelets and mommy-lets and omel-nats," I explain to Percy. He is sitting by his dish to watch me.

I pull out two long pink boxes of eggs and set them on the floor with the other food.

"What we need now, Percy, is some purple."

I have to hunt inside the fridge for the big jar of purple grape jelly. I love that purple stuff.

I can hold that purple grape jelly jar in one of my arms and take off the top with my other hand. So I do that now.

Plus, I can stick my finger in there and pull it out. And my finger turns purple. I bet you already guessed I do that now also.

Next, I stick my purple finger into my mouth to make sure this is the right grape jelly 'cause this is my secret part of my omel-nat. I suck all of the purple off my finger. And yep. This is the right grape jelly.

I slam the fridge door too hard, and things go very jiggly and jingly in there. "Shh-h-h," I warn Percy. I look fast at the door where my mom comes in from her bedroom. But she isn't there.

Not one bowl of my mom's has purple on it. So I pick a bowl that is kind of pinkish and put it on the counter. Then I move the foods up there on account of Percy is a snoop. That's what. Only I have to drag a chair over to the counter so I can reach everything.

I climb up on the chair and dump grape jelly into the pink bowl and pour in orange juice.

Plus also, I add the thick milk.

"Percy, we forgot the butter and cheese!" I have to climb down and tromp back to the fridge. "My granny forgets like this a hundred gazillion times when *she* makes *her* mommy-lets," I say.

This cooking is already fun. "Maybe, if I change my mind about being a movie star when I grow up, I could be a cook instead. Or maybe I'll be a cook who is a movie star. Or maybe a movie star who is a cook. What do you think, Percy?"

Percy swishes his tail back and forth, which is how cats think.

I need to mix up all of the stuff in the bowl. But I have to go through almost every single drawer in this place before I find that mixy *spit*-you-la thing for stirring up. It looks like a big white rubbery tongue on a stick. I love that thing when there's brownie batter on it or cookie batter from when Mom makes chocolate chip cookies.

While I mix up these foods, I sing very soft to keep Mommy and Daddy sleeping. "Ring around the omel-nats. Pockets full of roses." And "Twinkle, twinkle, omel-nats. How I wonder what you'll taste like."

Percy doesn't sing along.

I wish my bestest friend, Laurie, could be making these omel-nats with me. She knows all the words to funny songs. Except if Laurie came, we would have to call these things omel-Laurie-nats to be fair and square.

I mix up everything in the bowl. Only it stays very sloshy.

So I put in peanut butter. Peanut butter helps make everything not so sloshy.

Plus also, it makes everything smell peanut butterish.

But things are still kind of sloshy. And that's when I remember that I forgot something else. "Flour, Percy! You have to use that floury stuff for everything when you cook. Plus I forgot the sugar!"

I get the sugar that lives in the little sugar bowl on our table, and I dump it into my big bowl of peanut butter slosh.

"Now we need flour. How come we don't keep flour in a little flour bowl on our table like we keep sugar?" I ask Percy.

Percy does not answer.

I have to climb way up high from my chair to the counter to get the flour bag. It's on the highest shelf in our cupboard. Even when I'm standing on

the counter, I have to get on tiptoes just to touch
that giant flour bag. But the flour bag is way too big
to lift down. I think about this problem.

I think some more about this problem.

Percy hops up on the counter because I did it.
Percy is a copycat. Get it?

We are both thinking about this trouble. I need
that flour.

Then I get an idea. "I'll just slide the flour out
of the cupboard and off its shelf. That's what."

I reach on tiptoes, grab that flour, and slide it
out of the cupboard.

Splat!

Very much splat!

The flour sack smashes on the floor.

The bag tears wide open. White flour stuff goes
all over the place.

Percy jumps off the counter and hides under the
table.

I sneeze.

Percy copycats me.

I look at the door where my mom comes in.
She's still not.

"Now look what you did, Percy," I say. But it

was really the flour's fault. So I say sorry to Percy. He comes out of hiding.

I scoop up the parts of the flour that are not touching the ground. "See how I'm only taking the clean flour, Percy?" I say. "I can do this with snow also." I put the clean flour into my pinkish bowl. "Cooking is very hard work."

Percy plays with the dirty flour while I stir the clean flour into my bowl of peanut butter and jelly and orange juice and thick milk. And guess what! Things are not sloshy anymore in the pink bowl. That's what.

"Now all I have to do is cook up everything," I explain to my cat. "And *poof!* I will have one-of-a-kind wonderful grape omel-nats!"

Chapter 2

Not So Wonderful Omel-Nats

I know I can't use the stove to cook my grape omel-nats 'cause there's fire and hot in that thing when you turn it on. Plus, my mom said so.

Most of the times we use the microwave anyway. When I was a little kid, I called it the miracle-wave. It still is one. And this is why. A microwave can make things turn hot fast, but it doesn't turn your hand burny hot when you touch it.

There aren't big fat rules about not touching the microwave. So I touch it and open it and put both long pink boxes of eggs inside. Then I get my pinkish bowl of mixed-up foods and push it inside with the egg boxes.

I have to close the door really fast so nothing falls out.

I have watched Mommy push these microwave buttons a hundred gazillion times. And some of those times, when I asked her nicely a hundred gazillion times, she let me push those buttons also.

"Here goes," I tell Percy.

I push the buttons. Numbers pop up in lights and make a tiny doorbell noise.

Then I push the *go* button, and the microwave engine purrs like Percy. Only louder.

I look at that kitchen door where my mom comes in. She's still not.

While my omel-nats are cooking, I sit on the floor and pet Percy. "Just think, Percy. Pretty soon Mommy and Daddy will come into the kitchen for their boring breakfasts. They will see my one-of-a-kind wonderful purple grape omel-nats. They will get very big in their eyes and shout, 'Natalie 24! What a wonderful surprise! Thank you for making one-of-a-kind grape omel-nats!'"

I can see this happening inside my head like a happy movie. In this happy movie, I am all smiley faced. "You're welcome, Mommy and Daddy," I say to them — on account of that's the nice way to do that one.

"Back to work," I tell Percy. I climb back up on the counter to get my mom's prettiest plates for our special breakfast. "Mommy loves these plates, Percy."

I am climbing down off the counter when …

Pop! Pop! Pop pop pop pop pop pop pop pop pop pop!

I drop the plates and run for cover.

Percy runs for cover too, just like a copycat, because of that popping. Plus also that *crash, crash, cracking*.

We hide from all those *pop pops* under our breakfast table. I'm glad Percy is here with me 'cause that makes me not alone. Mommy runs into the kitchen, then slides to a stop. "What happened? What's going on?" she yells.

My heart is very thumpy.

"Mommy!" I cry from where I am still hiding with Percy.

"Natalie, are you all right?" Mommy rushes over to see for herself. "What happened, Nat? What was that noise?"

My mom doesn't have on her sleepy eyes. She is very big in her eyes, which are brown eyes like my eyes are brown. Only her hair is blondish, and my hair is blackish. Plus, her hair goes where it's supposed to go.

Except for now.

"Nat?" She is still peeking under the table at Percy and me.

My heart stops being so thumpy. But I would feel safer if Mommy would be a copycat like Percy and hide under this table with us. "Come under here with us," I whisper to her.

Mom stays where she is, staring at Percy and me. "Nat, what was that popping sound?"

My brain starts thinking.

And it is thinking that the *pop pop* came from the microwave. My purple grape omel-nats are in there! "Oh, no!"

"Nat?"

I crawl out from under the table. "My omel-nats! Are my omel-nats okay?"

"Your what?"

I run to the microwave and open up the door.

Gooey stuff plops out. Plus little pieces of white hard things. And yellow slime. And purplish gooey.

"Nat, what did you do?" Mom demands.

My neck feels all chokey on account of this messy stuff is not wonderful, purple grape omel-nats.

My dad stumbles into the kitchen. He still has his sleepy eyes on. "What's going on in here?" he asks. He yawns.

Then he gets big in his eyes.

His mouth opens up big, but nothing comes out for a minute. Then it does. "Oh man!" Daddy shouts. "Look at this kitchen!"

I do that.

That white flour is mostly piled in the middle part of the floor. But Percy footprints are all over the place.

There are white Percy prints on the floor.

White Percy prints on the counter.

And some of those white footprints look like they are people footprints from little people feet.

Plus also, there are other messy things around here when you look at the kitchen. There's a little orange puddle from orange juice that missed the bowl when I was pouring it in. Squishy purple grape jelly is on the floor and the cupboard. Percy tries to help and starts licking up the thick milk spilled on the counter.

Mom walks over to the microwave and stares at the goo inside. "Natalie, did you put eggs in this microwave?"

"You *gotta* put eggs in omel-nats!" I tell her. Maybe she doesn't know that about making real omelets. Because most things *she* puts into that microwave are already dinner, only all frozen. You don't put eggs in with frozen dinners.

Mommy shakes her head and stares into the microwave like she's waiting for something scary to come out of it.

My stomach feels twitchy.

I feel chokey in my neck.

"I'm sorry," I say. And I mean this part. "I only wanted to make onc-of-a-kind wonderful grape omel-nats." I feel tears in my head leaking out.

Daddy makes a funny, gurgley noise.

Mommy twirls around to him fast. "You think this is funny?" she asks him.

Daddy gets wrinkly in his face. "No, honey. I'll help clean up."

"No. Go back to bed. I'll handle this," Mom says.

Daddy's face looks a little happy. "Are you sure?" he asks my mom.

She nods. She doesn't look at Daddy because she is staring at the plates that broke themselves into pieces when I had to let them go so I could help Percy hide under the table.

I still feel chokey. "I'm sorry," I say very soft.

"I know," Mommy says. She lets the air out of her mouth like a leaky balloon.

Mommy holds her head in her own two hands like she is thinking her head could fall off.

I can only just barely hear what Mommy is saying to herself while she is holding her head. But I hear this much:

"Only Natalie."

Chapter 3

Not Very Interesting

"Go get dressed, Natalie," Mom says, not looking at me. She is still looking at the messed-up kitchen.

At preschool, we do cleanup by ourselves. I think my mom really wants to do kitchen cleanup by *her*self.

This is okay with me because cleanup is boring.

I pick up my blankie off the floor because it came to the kitchen this morning with me and Percy, even though I'm too much of a big girl to really have a blankie. Percy loves my blankie though.

"Natalie, go to the bathroom and wash up before you get dressed," Mom says.

I take my blankie into the bathroom and turn on the light.

Our walls in this bathroom are very boring and no fun. There are some pictures of flowers on the wallpaper. Only all the pictures are black and white, black lines on white paper, like coloring books nobody colored in.

Next to the sink we keep a short footstool
for standing up on so you can see yourself in the
mirror. Plus also, you can spit out your toothpaste
and it makes it into the sink if you're up there on
the footstool, and not so much if you're not up
there.

I step on the footstool. The second I see myself
in the mirror, I laugh my head off 'cause my face is
all powdery with flour stuff. Even some of my hair

is like that too. That's what.

I stare at me in the mirror, and I think this is
what I could look like when I'm a hundred years
old, like my granny. White hair and little all over
again.

Not too bad for a hundred years old.

When I splash water on my face, the flour turns
into paste. But it wipes off with towels.

I take off my PJs, and it snows flour in the
bathroom, which makes our bathroom a little fun
for a change.

Then I remember that my mom probably won't
think flour snow in the bathroom is fun. So I try to
wipe up the flour with towels. But doing this just
swooshes more white around.

I get my PJs wet and go to work wiping up the
white flour snow. Only I forgot about that paste
thing that happens between flour and water when
you mix them up together.

Sometimes if you make a mess, you can come
back to it later and it's all cleaned up. I run to my
bedroom and hope this happens.

When I come out to the kitchen, I'm wearing
purple shorts. Plus also, I'm wearing a purple T-shirt.

"Can Laurie come over and play?" I ask Mom. I really, really really want my bestest friend, Laurie, to come over. I am very lucky because my best friend lives on my street. Laurie has two sisters who are not fun, so she always wants to come play with me at my house.

Mommy wipes her face with her arm and doesn't answer me yet. My poor mom has a sweaty head from cleaning up so hard. Plus her hair is powdery. And it looks like flour and sweat work just like flour and water when it comes to making paste. I decide to remember that in case I'm ever in a desert that has flour and no water in it and I want some paste. Sweat plus flour makes paste.

I still don't have an okay or a yes, so I ask again. "Can she? Can Laurie come over and play?"

"Not today, Nat," Mom says.

"But I *need* Laurie today!" I say. Because it feels like I do.

Mom makes her eyes into little lines. "I think this might be a good day to be by yourself and think about what you did to my kitchen," she says.

I do not think this is a good idea.

I think having my bestest friend, Laurie, come

over and play is a very much better idea.

"Please?" I ask. Because I can't remember if I said that magic word before when I asked. I cross all of my fingers that I can make crossed. And I say that magic word again. Only I say it harder. "*Please?*"

"I said no," Mom answers.

I knew that word wasn't magic.

I uncross all of my fingers.

Mommy hands me the thick milk box. "Here. Throw this away, please."

I toss the milk box into the wastebasket. And somehow, that gives me a really good idea. "Mommy, can Jason come over and play?" I think this is a super idea. Jason could help me come up with my one-of-a-kind wonderful plan. Because so far this is not so much of a one-of-a-kind wonderful day.

"Please?" I say, not because that word has magic in it, but because I'm supposed to stick it in there when I ask for stuff.

"Natalie, I already said you couldn't have a friend over." My mom sounds tired out and a little mixed up, like she forgot what she really said before.

So I remind her. "You said, 'No, *Laurie* can't come over and play today.' You didn't say anything about Jason."

"All right. No, *Jason* can't come over and play today," Mommy says. "And no, *nobody else* can either. How's that?"

I think she isn't really asking me "How's that?" I don't think she really wants to know how I think that is that I can't have anybody come over and play. I think it is stinky. That's what.

Later, for lunch, Mom makes me a peanut butter and grape jelly sandwich. This is my favorite sandwich. So this is a nice thing, and I say thank you. But it is very not interesting or fun to eat this sandwich by myself.

After lunch I find Percy. He's curled up into a white sleeping ball on Dad's chair.

"Let's play baby, Percy." I try to pick up sleeping Percy.

Percy slides out of my hands like an old blankie.

Percy hates playing baby, even when he's awake.

"Want to go outside in the backyard?" I ask my cat.

Percy curls back up into a white sleeping ball. Sometimes Percy is just an old cat.

Mom is washing the microwave in the kitchen when I walk in. "Mommy, do you want to play with me outside?" I ask, trying not to let my voice do that up and down thing my mom calls whining.

"I'm pretty busy, Nat," Mom says, pointing to the microwave.

I drag my feet and the rest of me back to my bedroom. There is nothing fun to do by myself in here. I bend myself down so I can see under my bed. Under my bed is not scary in the daytime, in case you wonder about it.

I reach under there and come out with my Old Maid cards. I forgot all about these cards. Laurie and I used to play Old Maid like crazy.

I race back to the kitchen with my old cards. "Mommy!" I shout.

Mom drops a bag of apples. "Natalie? What's wrong?"

"I found my Old Maid cards! Do you want to play Old Maids with me?" I make a giant smiley face at her.

"I'm sorry, honey," she says. "I need to make some calls."

That's what my mom does for her work. She makes phone calls all of the time. Before I was born, Mom was a big boss over a whole lot of people in a work office. Now she mostly just bosses Daddy and me. But sometimes she gets to boss businesspeople over the telephone. She is a home worker of business. And this is because I was born and she wanted to be at home because that's where I was.

Daddy is still a business worker away from home.

I check on Percy. But Percy is still a sleeping ball. Plus, he doesn't know how to play Old Maid.

I drag myself back to my bedroom and dig out other stuff from under my bed.

Blocks. But blocks aren't interesting without Jason building them so high they fall down on us.

Dolls. But dolls aren't too much fun, even when Laurie and I play them.

Books. Books are usually very interesting *and* fun, only not today.

Puzzles. Puzzles are hard by myself. Plus many pieces of these puzzles are not there anyway.

I give up on my room and find my mom talking on the phone in her office that is in our house. She is saying stuff like this:

"Do you have the numbers on that?"

"I'll see what I can do."

"Tell them I'll have the report by Tuesday."

"Blah. Blah. Blah."

My mom gets very aggravated at me if I talk to her at the same time she's talking to people on the phone. Aggravated is what other mothers call mad. So I just stand and watch her talk, even though this is not interesting or fun. We are not allowed to say "boring" in our house, or I would call this boring too. That's what.

I see a bunch of those silvery wire paper clips on her desk, and some are clipped over papers. So I play with those a little.

"Blah. Blah. Blah," Mom says to the phone again. She takes the papers with paper clips away from me.

Maybe if I just whisper, Mom won't get aggravated. "Mom," I say soft, "will you play horsey with me?"

She makes a long, puffy sound. Then she tells the phone, "Let me call you back in a minute."

My heart gets thumpy because I think my mom is going to play horsey with me. And that's why she has to call that person on the phone back.

"I get to be the horse rider!" I shout first.

Mommy picks up the phone again and pushes buttons. "Hi, Marge," she says.

Now my heart is really thumpy. I know who Marge is.

"Marge," Mom says, looking at me while she talks to the phone, "Can Laurie come over and play with Natalie?"

"Yippee!" I shout. Because this is the most one-of-a-kind wonderful thing that has happened today.

Chapter 4

Between the Lines

I sit outside on our step to wait for my bestest friend, Laurie. My mom came up with this great idea for me to go wait outside.

Only I think I must have been waiting out here forever.

Three cars drive by.

A bunch of big girls on big bikes ride by, laughing at each other.

Laurie is not in those cars. Or on those bikes.

I stare down the sidewalk where Laurie will come walking up from her house. Her mom will come walking with her. Or maybe one of her big sisters will come with her because Laurie's mom makes them do things like that with Laurie sometimes.

"Nat!"

I know before I look that my bestest friend yelled my name.

"Laurie!" I yell back, like I haven't seen her for a hundred gazillion years.

"Nat!" Laurie yells back, like she hasn't seen me for a hundred gazillion years.

Laurie has on purple shorts and a T-shirt that has words on it and a bear. Her hair is yellow and curly all over the place.

"I'll come back for you before dinner," says Laurie's mom. She kisses the top of Laurie's yellow head. "Be good now."

Laurie's mom stands up straight, and she goes up a long way because she is a tall mom. "Hi, Natalie," she says, smiling down at me. "Why don't you girls go tell your mother that Laurie's here, okay?"

We run inside my house and do that.

After Laurie's mom walks back home, mine gives Laurie and me some celery with peanut butter in it. Then she goes back on her telephone. And I don't even care this time.

Laurie and I go outside and lick our peanut butter out of our celeries while we swing on swings in the backyard. There are birds out here. But not Percy.

"I love birds," Laurie says.

"Me too," I agree.

When there is no more peanut butter left in my celery, I ask Laurie, "Do birds like celery?"

Laurie looks at her own celery. There's no peanut butter left in her celery either. "I think so," she answers.

"Me too," I agree.

We give our celery to the birds. They save it for later.

I tell Laurie all about my not so wonderful grape omel-nats. Plus also, I tell her how Peter pulled my hair yesterday in the grocery store. And a not so nice girl named Sasha laughed when Peter did that.

At all the right times, Laurie says these things: "They shouldn't have done that."

And, "Peter can be a mean teaser."

And, "That Sasha is a very not nice girl sometimes."

And, "That wasn't fair!"

And the last thing she says is, "I wonder how God can love everybody."

And that is a very true thing that I also wonder.

"Laurie," I say, when we are done with swinging, "I *need* to do a one-of-a-kind wonderful thing today."

Laurie nods her head like she knows this is true and that she was already thinking the exact same thing.

"I'm all out of wonderful ideas," I tell her.

Laurie is quiet for one minute. Then she gets very big in her eyes. "We could color!"

I do not think coloring is so very wonderful.

But Laurie loves to color. She's really good at coloring. She can stay between the lines and everything.

I can't stay between those lines. Ever. Those lines are always too close together for my crayons.

Sometimes it makes me sad in my heart when I can't color in between the lines and Laurie *can* color between the lines.

But she is my best friend. And so even though I can't stay in the lines with her, I say, "Okay. Let's color."

We run to my mom's office. "Mom, where are my coloring books?" I ask.

She is talking on her phone. She holds up her wait-a-minute finger.

I wait a whole minute or maybe a million billion minutes until Mom stops talking.

"Your crayons are in your room, Natalie," Mom says. I think she sounds a little aggravated. But she is still kind of smiley because Laurie is with me. Mommies are always smilier to other people's kids.

"But I don't know where my crayons are in my room," I tell her.

"Look for them, Nat," Mom says.

"Where?" I ask. Because looking for things is even harder than coloring between the lines. Plus, mommies always know where things are without any looking.

Mommy makes that balloon-leaking noise.

Then she gets up from her phone chair and walks to my room.

Laurie and I have to run to follow her. Laurie is a very good runner like me.

My mom marches straight over to my dresser, where my clothes live when they aren't on me. She opens the last door to my dresser.

And those coloring books are right in there.

Laurie and I both tell Mom thank you. Laurie says it first. And so do I, almost.

"Better wash up before you start coloring your pictures," Mom says. "Your hands are a mess."

I look at my hands and Laurie's hands. They are not a mess. They just have peanut butter on them.

We go into the bathroom. Even our plain old bathroom with white wallpaper and black lines for flower pictures is fun with Laurie in it.

I stand up on the footstool and turn on the water.

Laurie stands up on the footstool too. We are side by side. Laurie has on her purple shorts. I have on my purple shorts. And we are the only things not black and white in this whole entire bathroom.

We jiggle the footstool with our feet. That makes Laurie laugh. And that makes me laugh.

We are both laughing and pushing our hands under the water when I look up at the boring white and black wallpaper.

And that's when I get an idea starting in my head.

It's a one-of-a-kind wonderful idea.

"Laurie!" I say, my heart all thumpy. "Let's color the bathroom!"

Chapter 5

A Wonderful, Colorful Idea

"Color the bathroom?" Laurie squeals. "Wow! Can we, Nat?" I can tell by how she says this that her heart is all thumpy like mine.

We run back to my bedroom and get my biggest box of colors. The box says there are 64 colors inside.

Sasha has a box of crayons with a gazillion colors in it. I saw this for myself at preschool when she was showing them off.

Laurie pushes back the lid of my coloring box. "You have a lot of crayons missing, Nat."

I peek inside. There are empty places all over this box. Plus also, some of the crayons are broken. "I think there are still 24 colors left," I guess.

Laurie giggles. "24 is the perfect number of crayons to color a bathroom with." Laurie also loves the number 24.

But it is not her lucky number or her middle name.

We race back to the bathroom and close the door with us on the inside with those 24 colors.

Laurie sets the box of colors on the sink and opens the lid. She stares at the purple crayon.

I stare at the purple crayon. It isn't as big as the other crayons even though it's not broken. And that is because I use that color a whole lot.

Laurie takes the purple crayon out of the box.

I feel that chokey thing in my neck when she takes that color.

I very much love purple.

"Here. You take purple, Nat," Laurie says. She hands me the purple crayon.

"Are you sure?" I ask. "*You* can have it."

"I'll take this one." She reaches into the color box and comes out with a color that is purplish. But not purple.

I love my bestest friend, Laurie. "Thanks," I say. "Hey! We can trade off!"

Laurie nods. Then she starts right in coloring on a big flower. She colors very slow, so it is a little boring to keep watching her.

I pick out a flower I can reach without standing on the footstool. This flower will be so beautiful when it turns purple.

I color and color.

I get more and more excited coloring this flower and imagining it beautiful.

I think about my mom and dad seeing this beautiful colored flower and being surprised and saying, "Why, Natalie 24! What a one-of-a-kind wonderful flower!"

I color faster and faster and faster.

My purple color moves over to another flower that's next to that other flower. And I keep coloring.

I am coloring super fast now. More and more flowers are turning purple.

"How do you like it, Nat?" Laurie asks. She is looking at her own purplish, but not purple, flower.

Laurie's flower is perfect, with all its purplish color right inside those black lines.

"Wow!" I say.

Laurie looks over at my purple flowers. "Yours are good too," she says.

Only now I'm getting a real look at my flowers. And they are all a big blob of purple. One big, giant blob of purple.

Not so much flowers.

I think about my mom looking at this big blob of purple where flowers used to be. This makes my stomach feel twitchy. And not in a good kind of way.

"You are so lucky, Nat," Laurie says. She puts her purplish crayon back in the box and takes out a pink one. Then she starts coloring the next flower. "*My* mom would never let *me* color her wall."

"Really?" I think about this new thought. Laurie's mom is a nice mom.

She's a lot like *my* mom.

"Really," Laurie says. "Sarah told me that once she got some of her lipstick junk on a towel and my mom went crazy." Sarah is Laurie's big sister who isn't too much fun, but is still kind of nice. "Mom told her she'd better get that towel clean, or else."

"Lipstick and crayons aren't the same things. And towels are not the same things as walls," I say.

"Sarah and Mom put the lipstick towel in the washing machine. That helped a little," Laurie explains. "But Mom was still pretty mad."

Walls don't fit in washing machines.

I take a towel off its hanger and rub on the purple I colored where flowers were. That purple stays where it is, except a little gets on the towel.

There is a knocking on the bathroom door.

I jump so much that I drop my purple crayon and also the towel.

"Natalie? Are you in there?" Mom shouts.

Something on the inside of me feels like saying no.

"Natalie?" Mom shouts.

"I'm here," I say not so loud.

"Where's Laurie?" Mom asks through the bathroom door.

"I'm here too!" Laurie shouts.

"What are you girls doing in there?" Mom asks.

"Coloring." This word comes out of me very soft.

"What?" Mom shouts.

"Coloring," I say even softer.

"Honey, I can't hear you," Mom says.

"We're coloring!" Laurie shouts.

"Oh," Mom says. Then there is a lot of quiet outside that door.

I think my mom has gone back to her phone.

I am wrong.

"Did you say coloring?" Mom asks. "Why are you coloring in there?" Her voice sounds funny.

The doorknob turns.

The door opens.

Mommy screams.

Laurie drops her pink crayon.

My insides get twitchier.

"It's … a … surprise," I say. I want to say that it's a one-of-a-kind wonderful surprise. Only Mom's face makes me not say this. I can tell already that she is very much surprised. But she does not think purple is so wonderful.

My mom calls Laurie's mom, and Laurie's mom comes to get Laurie.

When Mommy shows her the colored bathroom flowers, Laurie's mom covers up her mouth with her hand. I think that hand is trying to keep a laugh inside there.

Because my mom says, "Don't laugh, Marge. It could have been your wall, you know."

Mom and I walk outside with Laurie and her mom.

On our front step, Laurie's mom turns and pats me on my head, in a nice way. Then she looks over at my mom and says, "Only Natalie."

Chapter 6

Thinking about That

Percy comes with me to my bedroom to think about what I did and why I should not have.

I think about that black and white bathroom.

I think about the color purple. And the color purplish. And purple blobs.

I think about Laurie coloring right in between those lines of flowers.

I think about me coloring very fast and outside of the lines.

I think about my mom screaming and calling Laurie's mom.

I think about Laurie's mom saying, "Only Natalie."

But all of this thinking is making me tired. I think I am all thought out. That's what.

Percy is sitting on my bed. I think he looks lonely.

Poor Percy is lonely on account of my mom and dad say NO every time I ask for another cat or a dog or a horsy that isn't plastic, or a frog, or a fish, or a snake (and I didn't mean that one), or a dolphin, or a penguin, or an ant.

I don't mean aunt like Laurie's Aunt Katy. I mean the teeny-tiny ants.

Sasha is a scaredy cat about those teeny-tiny ants.

In my Sunday school class once upon a time, that Sasha girl saw a teeny-tiny ant and screamed her head off. Peter, that boy who pulled my hair in the grocery store, ran over to where Sasha was screaming her head off. And he stepped very hard on that teeny-tiny ant. He killed it dead. That's what.

And that can make me sad in my heart if I think about that.

"I need to get you some friends," I say to my lonely cat, Percy. Percy is the only one to talk to in this place. Percy doesn't say anything back to me.

"We can play with my animals, Percy," I say anyway.

Percy doesn't say anything again.

I love my stuffed animals. I love them better than my dolls. Except for sometimes.

I reach under my bed until I feel something fuzzy.

And I come out with Steg-O! Steg-O is my little gray dinosaur that my dad gave me when I was so sick they made me have a sleepover in the hospital.

I hug my dinosaur. I love him very much, and he has been gone a really long time.

"Steg-O?" I say, glad that there's somebody besides Percy to talk to in here now. "Percy wants to play with you."

I put Steg-O on the bed next to Percy. Percy uncurls, then curls again.

I go back under my bed. And I find Brownie under there!

Brownie is my bear. He has been lost forever.

"I missed you!" I shout to Brownie. I hug my old bear. Then I cough 'cause Brownie has fuzzy dust on him. I put him on the other side of Percy.

My mom knocks on my door. Then she comes on in. "Everything okay in here, Natalie?" she asks.

I nod 'cause somewhere along the way everything began being okay. And I don't even know when that was.

"Good," Mom says. She has stopped looking so big in her eyes, and she has her regular face back.

Mom comes in the rest of the way. She walks

over to Percy and Brownie and Steg-O. "You found Brownie," she says.

"Yep. He was hiding under my bed," I explain.

She sits down next to me on the bed. "Did you think about what you did to the bathroom wall?" she asks.

"Yes. I'm sorry it made you scream, Mommy." And this is a true thing.

"I know you are, Nat," Mom says.

She puts her hand on my head. I really like how her hand on my head makes me feel better.

"I'm going to have to get new wallpaper now," Mom says.

"Because we colored on the old paper?" I ask. Putting paper on walls is a very big messy thing. I know because I saw my dad paste-up wallpaper in Mom's office.

"I'm sorry," I say. But now I feel sorrier than sorry. And thinking about this makes my neck chokey.

Plus also, I am sad in my heart. I don't like feeling sad in my heart.

My mom puts her arm around my shoulders. "Isn't it a great thing to know that God loves us no

matter what? I love you like that too, Nat. And God forgives both of us."

I think about this. And this is a very good thing to think about. It makes my throat less chokey. Plus also, it takes the sadness out of my heart.

Mom pets Percy, and that cat makes his rumbling noise. My mom knows just how to make Percy purr. "So, next time," Mom says, "how about thinking about things like coloring walls *before* you do it?"

I nod. This feels like it would be a helpful plan, but hard to remember.

"Well," she says, heading for my door, "I'm going to get dinner. You're welcome to come out of your room now."

"No thanks," I say. Now this room isn't boring like it used to be when I was in it alone.

When Mommy is gone, I dive back under my bed. And when I come back up, I have Whitey and Blackie and Orangey and Grayey. They are all kitties. But they aren't the real kind, like Percy. And they are those colors that are in their names.

I run to my dresser and take down Purpley, who is another fake cat. Then I pile up all those cats on the bed. And Percy is in the middle of that pile up.

I look at Percy. He is not purring, but he looks asleep.

I think he would love to be on top of that pileup.

I pick up Percy and lift him up very high. Higher than all the pretend cats. Higher than Steg-O and Brownie. "Here comes Percy!" I shout.

Percy wakes up too much. He wiggles and twists. Then he reaches out his paw and scratches my hand. "Ow! Bad Percy!" I let him go.

He prances right back to the bottom of my bed, all alone.

There's a white line on my hand where Percy scratched it. That line is almost bloody. I get off my bed and walk to my door. Then I turn around to make an aggravated face at Percy.

Percy is all curled up again.

"You better stay in here all by your own self and think about what you did," I tell my bad cat, Percy.

And when I walk away, I shake my head and say, "Only Percy."

Chapter 7

Bounce, Bounce, Bounce

My mom is not in the kitchen when I come out, even though this is where she usually is when she tells me she's going to get dinner.

She is also not getting dinner in the living room, which is a funny name to call that room. We live in all of our rooms.

I find my mom in her office. She's on her phone.

I wave at her.

She waves at me. Her wave is the kind that says, "Not now, Nat."

"Blah, blah, blah," Mommy says into her phone.

I go looking for Percy, but he is not in my room anymore. He probably got bored thinking about what he did.

"Percy?" I call. I walk down the hallway, and I call some more. "Percy? Percy?"

Percy doesn't answer.

I go into my mom and dad's bedroom. They share and share alike in here.

They share a great big bed with a flowery cover on it. I have to climb to get up on that bed. And I do that right now.

This is a very good jumping bed.

I take off my shoes so I won't hurt the bed. Then I jump.

I jump and jump and jump.

Maybe I can bounce a wonderful idea out of my head.

I bounce and bounce and bounce.

Nothing wonderful comes out. I let my bottom hit the bed. The rest of me stops bouncing.

I sit on the big bed and let my feet hang over the

side. And I am looking right into Daddy's closet.
I hop off the bed and go look closer up. My dad's
closet has a sliding door that slides back and forth.
Open and close. Slide and slide.

So I do that a while until it stops being fun.

There are a gazillion shirts and coats in my
dad's closet. He has to wear these nice clothes
when he goes to his office. But when he comes
home, he wears his regular daddy clothes.

And his regular daddy shoes.

I try to count my dad's shoes, but they get
mixed up. And my mom has even more shoes than
my dad. That's what.

I kneel on the floor and try to count my dad's
shoes again. He may only have two feet, but he still
has many, many shoes.

Shoes for going running.

Shoes for going walking.

Shoes for cutting grass and getting dirty.

Shoes for going to the office in.

And two shoes he puts on to go to church.
These shoes are black with nothing on them.

I pick up these two shoes and sit down with
them in my lap.

When I go to church, I get to wear my shiny white shoes with a buckle on the top. Or purple shoes if I had purple shoes.

My church shoes are the fanciest shoes in my whole room.

Poor Daddy's church shoes are not fancy at all. They are the plainest shoes in his whole room. In fact, they are boring shoes. That's what.

I love my daddy. He should have one-of-a-kind wonderful shoes to go to church in.

I stare at Daddy's boring plain shoes. And just like that I get a one-of-a-kind wonderful idea!

Chapter 8

Sticky Church Shoes

My heart gets very thumpy as I run back to my
bedroom.

I have to throw out coloring books and socks
and toy horses, but finally I find what I'm looking
for. My stickers! My stickers are full of color and
fanciness.

I got these stickers from my granny. She got
them in the mail from the postman lady.

Some of these stickers have flags of America on
them.

Some of these stickers have pictures of kitties
and dogs my granny saved from getting killed. She
sent money to people who rescue pets that nobody
wants, and so they sent her these stickers.

Other stickers are sparkly yellow smiley faces.

My granny got these sparkly smiley faces so she
could give me one every time I was really, really
good at her house. She didn't use up many of those
stickers. So she just gave me the whole big bag of
them.

I run back to Mom and Dad's bedroom with all
of my stickers. On the floor in front of the closet sit
Daddy's plain black church shoes. I pick up one of
those shoes and start stickering.

I put flags on the toe.

I put kitties on one side of the shoe.

I put puppies on the other side.

I stick sparkly smiley faces all over the top.

Then I do all that stickering on the other shoe
until there's almost no shoe left.

When I think I'm all done, I see some star stickers I forgot about. So I put those on the inside of the shoes so my daddy's church shoes will be wonderful inside and outside.

My dad will have the most wonderful church shoes in our whole entire church. He will walk into church, and people will say, "What one-of-a-kind wonderful shoes you have!"

And my dad will feel very good about this. He might even tell those people, "Why, my daughter, Natalie 24, made these shoes wonderful for me."

I look at the shoes again, and there's no more room for even one more sticker. But I still have some cats left. So I put stickers on the bottoms of those shoes.

And they are perfect. That's what. I can hardly wait for Daddy to see these wonderful shoes I made for him.

I hear the front door open up and close again. My heart gets thumpy. *Daddy's home!*

I can hear my mom going to meet my dad in our living room. "Natalie?" she shouts. "Daddy's home!"

I stand up. My stomach is all twitchy in a good way. I can't wait to show off the sticker shoes.

I stick my two feet into Daddy's big, fancy shoes and head for the living room.

"Nat, honey?" Daddy calls. "Where are you?"

"Coming!" I shout.

It's not easy to walk in these big shoes, even with all the stickers on them. But I want Daddy to see his wonderful shoes walking. So I keep scooting and shuffling down the hall, around the corner, and all the way to the living room.

Mom and Dad are talking to each other with their backs to me. At the same time, they turn around.

"Guess what I did, Daddy!" I yell.

Nobody guesses. They are staring at the sticker shoes.

I give them a hint. "It's really wonderful!"

They still are not guessing this. They are still just staring at the sticker shoes.

"Look! I made your church shoes one-of-a-kind wonderful!" I yell.

Dad and Mom are still staring at my feet.

I scoot all the way up to them so they can get a better look. Then I kick up one foot so one sticker shoe falls off. "Ta da!" I shout.

Daddy bends himself down and picks up the shoe.

He looks at it.

And looks at it.

He touches one of the flag stickers. Then he pulls at it, but it stays where it is.

"I stuck them on," I explain. My stomach is starting to feel twitchy, but not in a good way.

Daddy keeps picking at that flag until part of it, the colored part, comes off. His face looks sad. "They're really stuck on there," he says.

I nod and look over at my mom. She still hasn't said anything. But her face isn't sad like Daddy's face. She has one hand over her mouth, like Laurie's mom did when she was trying to hold a laugh inside her mouth.

"Welcome to my world," Mom says. She walks away fast, out to the kitchen.

Welcome to my world? I think that's a funny thing to say. Why would Mommy welcome Daddy to her world? It's *our* world, and my dad lives in it with the rest of us already.

Mom must realize that what she said was a funny thing to say too 'cause she starts laughing her head off in the kitchen.

"How do you like your one-of-a-kind wonderful, fancy church shoes, Daddy?" I ask.

"What?"

I hope my daddy isn't getting old ears like Granny's.

"Your church shoes!" I say very loud.

Only Daddy doesn't even look up from his shoe. He keeps pick, pick, picking at those stick, stick, stickers.

I look at all the smiley faces on those fancy shoes. Then I look at my dad's face. It is *not* a smiley face.

It is a frowny face.

"Daddy?" I say because my stomach is bad twitchy now.

Daddy is not saying anything to me.

But he is saying something to the shoe.

Or to himself.

And he is saying this something over and over.

Finally, I figure out what my daddy is saying.

He is saying, "Only Natalie."

Chapter 9

Backyard Friends

We have to eat dinner. So I don't get to go to my room to think about what I did to Daddy's church shoes.

Even dinner is not so wonderful. Mommy says it's "goo-lush." It looks and tastes just like it sounds.

"What a wonderful dinner!" Daddy says anyway.

Wonderful? This does not feel like a fair thing. I'm the one who wanted to do something wonderful.

"How about some dessert?" Mom asks. But she just brings out a bowl of gooey fruits mixed up together instead of real dessert.

"No, thank you," I say nicely, 'cause even Percy knows fruits aren't dessert. Brownies are dessert.

After I help put dishes in the sink, Percy and I go to the backyard.

I sit on the swing.

But it gets boring fast without Laurie swinging

in that other swing.

I drag my feet to make the swing stop swinging. I like when the swing flops around crooked.

But I don't like it enough to keep doing it forever.

Percy walks off. But he was already kind of boring. He hates swinging.

I look up at the sky, and it's pretty wild. I like looking at this crazy sky. The sun is behind a fat black cloud that keeps growing and growing.

Other clouds are moving fast, racing each other. This sky is looking like a spooky Halloween sky. That's what.

I stop looking up there.

I walk around in our backyard and try not to think about anything. But my brain is trying to think about all of the one-of-a-kind wonderful things I thought I was doing today and how none of those things turned out wonderful.

I kick a rock to the back of my backyard, by the fence our neighbors made to keep me out of their yard. And that's when I see something.

I almost step on it. But my foot stops just in time.

What I see is a little pile of dirt that makes my

I know what this pile is. It's smaller than my hand is when I squeeze in my fingers. Pieces of dirt are piled up and look like a tiny Eskimo igloo.

Only it's black instead of white.

And it's not freezing cold.

And it's made of dirt instead of snow and ice cubes.

"Ants," I whisper, "and an ant house!"

I squat down so I can see these ants better. It makes me remember how Peter stomped on that ant when Sasha was scared of it. Plus also, he says he

stomps on whole ant houses.

I stare at the long line of real live ants. Almost every ant in that line is carrying something. Most of them have a piece of dirt. And others of the ants have bigger stuff, like pieces of cat food or maybe dog food.

They are working hard and carrying everything to their ant house.

In the tiny ant house, there are holes exactly like the windows and doors in my house. Only they're tinier. And made out of dirt. I watch the line of ants going in the windows and doors of their house. And I watch more ants coming out of those windows and doors too.

I keep watching those ants and wondering how God can make something so tiny. And how come they know how to build a nice ant house like this.

And I think, yeah, ants might be easier to make than birds or camels or maybe kangaroos or horses, and even people. But still, I think God did a really good job on ants.

Percy comes over and sniffs at those working ants God made and put in my backyard.

"Go away, Percy!" I shout, because I don't want

my cat to squish the ant house.

Percy prances away. I watch more ants bring stuff to their ant house, and I start to love these ants and their ant home.

"What you guys need are names," I tell them. "You're Blackie. And you can be Brownie. And Anty, Tiny, Teeny, and Bug."

Pretty soon I run out of any names, and there are still a gazillion ants left. So I make them go by the same names, with a little difference.

"Blackie 24.

"Brownie 24.

"Anty 24.

"Tiny 24.

"Teeny 24.

"Bug 30-11." I make that name different on account of I don't like the name Bug 24.

I wish Laurie could be here with me. She knows many ant names.

I try again to make up what names those ants go by. "Sasha," I say, pointing at an ant that looks like it would laugh if somebody pulled another ant's hair.

"Peter," I say, pointing at an ant that looks like

he would pull some ant's hair.

Only I take back that name of Peter because saying that name makes me remember how the real Peter stepped on an ant and killed it dead. And that makes me sadder than it did the first time, now that I have so many ant friends.

I keep watching, and the ants keep building their wonderful ant house.

The sky rumbles and shakes up the ants and me.

We are a little scared.

But the ants keep working. So I keep watching.

The sky rumbles and roars much bigger this time. I want to run inside. Only I'm worried about these little anty guys.

A big, fat glob of raindrop plops on my arm.

Then another glob drops in the dirt, just missing the ant house.

Then one more rain glob plops on my head.

I look at the ground and see dark, wet spots.

Then I see a big glob of rain splat right on top of the ant house.

"Stop it!" I tell the rain.

But another raindrop plops on the ant house. Then another. And another.

Blackie and Brownie go very fast into that ant house. And Tiny 24 and Teeny 24 walk crooked outside the ant house, like they forgot where their house is.

There's a big fat crash in the sky. It's thunder.

More raindrops fall on the ant house. The window holes close up. The roof sags down. Their whole house is getting ruined.

"Get out!" I shout at the ants. I'm scared that the whole ant house is falling down, and I'm scared all the ants will get smushed by their own house. Smushed dead. Or with broken heads.

I have to do something. I know I can't leave them out here to get their heads smushed.

And then I know something else.

Something one-of-a-kind wonderful.

I will save these ants!

Chapter 10

Ants in Your Plants

Thunder is booming. Rain is plopping down on us faster and faster.

As quick as I can, I scoop up those ants and put them inside the pocket of my purple shorts. Then I scoop up more ants into my other pocket of my purple shorts.

Then I remember that I'm wearing my baseball hat that goes with my baseball shirt with the 24 on it. I scoop up as much ant house as I can fit inside my hat. Plus also some more ants.

"Come on, Blackie and Brownie and Anty and Blackie 24, and you other ants!" I shout.

The sky is shouting louder than me.

So I go louder than the sky. "Nat 24 to the rescue! I'll save you!"

What I'm doing is a wonderful ant saving. And it makes me happy in my heart to do that job.

I run very fast across my backyard.

I run very fast through the backyard door to my house.

I run very fast through the kitchen, where nobody is.

Then I stop running very fast.

I am very drippy.

Teeny and Brownie 24, and Blackie, and their families are drippy too.

I can't hold on to these drippy things forever in my pockets and baseball hat. But where does an ant saver put saved ants? That's what I'd like to know. There's no good place for saved ants in the whole entire kitchen.

Not in the cereal cupboard.

Not in the fridge.

Not in the microwave.

Not under the table.

We run — the ants and me — to the bathroom. But there's no good place for ants in the bathroom. Plus, the wall is still colored purple.

I am a little shivery because it's cold when you're wet and you have ants in your pockets and hat.

I run into the living room and try not to drip as I look all around for a good spot.

That's when I see it! The perfect place for my ant friends!

My mom has plants in here. Big bowls of plants sit right on the floor in our living room. She takes very good care of her plants too. One of my mom's plants is bigger than I am. It has a special spot by the window and kinda behind a big chair so little kids can't knock it over so easy.

My mom loves her big plant.

She gives it water. She gives it food.

And, sometimes I see Mommy talking to that plant. And I'm not even making that part up.

The big plant is inside of a big fat plant bowl. And inside that plant bowl, there's dirt. That's what. Just like there was inside the ant house in the backyard.

"I've found you guys the perfect home," I tell Blackie and Brownie.

I have to jiggle myself behind the chair to get to the big plant. Then I have to empty my pockets. I pull out all the ants and the parts of their ant house out of my pockets. This is not as easy as it sounds, because it's very squishy in my pockets.

I pull out my pockets all the way and shake off any ants left. And I shake my hat full of ant house and ants.

Most of the ants go right into the big plant. Some of the ants look like they're sleeping already. That's how much this plant works like an ant house for them.

Other ants start right away crawling around in plant dirt on an explore. I think I see Blackie 24 climbing on a leaf.

I'm watching Blackie 24 when my mom walks into the living room. "Natalie?" she says.

I turn to Mom and smile very big.

"Look at you! You're a mess!" she shouts.

I can't stop smiling, though. I can hardly wait to tell her about the wonderful ant saving I just did. "Mommy, I — !" I start telling her. Only she won't let the words get out of my smiley mouth.

"Natalie Elizabeth, get out of the living room! You're filthy! Don't touch anything." She yells all of this while I'm trying to tell her about the ants. And she only calls me by that "Elizabeth" middle name, instead of my "24" middle name, when she is very, very aggravated.

"But, Mom. Here's what happened in the backyard when — "

"Now! Nat, get in the bathtub this minute!" Mommy is pointing to the bathroom like I don't know where that bathtub is and maybe that's why I'm not in it yet.

I cross the living room. My feet say *squish, squish* on the rug.

When I squish in front of my mom, she still has her pointy finger going. She has her line eyes on. And I think she is very much aggravated.

Maybe my mom should get done being aggravated before I tell her about the one-of-a-kind wonderful ant save.

I walk past my mom's pointy finger to the bathroom.

She comes in after me and turns on the bathtub water. Water splashes into the tub, and I love that noisy sound.

"Can I have bubbles?" I ask nicely with my smiley face.

"Not tonight," she answers without her smiley face. "And don't forget to scrub behind your ears, Natalie," she says for the gazillionth time.

"How come?" I ask, not being a smarty Alec, but just asking. It seems like there are lots much more important places I could spend my time besides behind my ears.

"Just do it," Mom says, sounding aggravated. "Please," she adds on because that's the nice way to ask. I think maybe she is aggravated 'cause her bathroom wall is purple and not between the lines.

She turns off the water and sits on the footstool. Then she closes her eyes on account of I am a little lady who needs her privacy. Or maybe she's tired.

I take off my wet and dirty clothes and climb into the bathtub. The water is warm and slurpy.

I breathe in a big bunch of air. Then I close my eyes and stuff my head under the water.

It's dark and wet down under the water.

Only I don't stay down there very long because you can't breathe down there. While I'm down there, the water behind my ears does all the scrubbing by itself.

I like my bath so much that I almost forget about that wonderful thing I did for those ants.

But then I hear my daddy shout, "Kelly! Come to the living room! We've got ants!"

Chapter 11

One-of-a-Kind Horrible

"Ants? Don't be crazy. We don't have ants."
Mom's voice is very loud like Daddy's. She lifts
me out of the bathtub and gives me a towel. Then
she runs out of the bathroom, down the hall, and to
the living room.

Mommy screams.

"They're over here too," Daddy says.

"They can't be!" Mom shouts.

My tummy is very twitchy and bubbly.

But I know those ants can't be *my* ants. I only
put ants into my mom's big plant, not on the floor.

"Bill, we have ants on our chair!" Mom shouts.
"Get them!"

Bill is the other name my dad goes by. He
shouts back, "They're everywhere, Kelly!"

Kelly is the other name my mom goes by.

Now my stomach is for sure twitchy in a bad way.

I put on my PJs by myself. The 24 on the back
of my PJs is sticking to my back because the towel
didn't reach that back water.

The bathroom floor is slippy slidey on account of all the water that fell on it. But I hurry out of there anyway.

The first thing I see in the living room is this funny thing. Mom and Dad are on the floor like they're playing horsy. And both of them are the horsies.

But this is only funny for a little bit. Then

my mom turns around. Her face is aggravated. "Natalie, don't come in here, honey."

"How come?" I ask.

"Ants," Daddy says. He doesn't turn around. He grabs at something on the floor.

"Ants?" I ask, my stomach twisting and bubbling.

"I just can't believe this!" Mom says in a cry voice. "I've never had ants."

"Ants aren't so bad," I say.

"They are if they're in your house," Daddy says. He reaches in front of him on the floor and swats at something. "Got one."

"Daddy!" I scream. "Don't!"

They turn around and look at me now.

"Don't kill Blackie! Or Brownie 24." I have cry in my voice too. And it is coming out now.

"Blackie?" Mom asks. "Brownie 24? Wh-what are you talking about, Natalie?"

Daddy gets up on his feet. His eyes are lines. "Natalie Elizabeth?" Daddy almost never calls me by that "Elizabeth" middle name. "What do you know about these ants?"

"God made them," I say very soft.

"Nat?" Daddy says.

"I only wanted them to stay alive," I tell them.

"And I only put those ants in Mom's big plant. Not anyplace else."

"My plant?" Mom says. "*This* plant?" She points her pointy finger at it.

I nod my head in the yes way. "Because dirt is what those ants like best in an ant house."

"You brought ants inside the house?" Mom acts like she can't quite believe this is the truth.

"I only wanted them to be alive in your plant. Not on your floor. Not on your chair." I look down at my feet, and two ants are climbing onto my toe. I don't recognize these ants. "Maybe these ants that aren't in your big plant aren't *my* ants."

Mom gets to her feet and stands up next to my dad.

It feels like an unfair thing. There are two on their side.

There's only me on my side.

"Natalie Elizabeth!" Mom and Dad say at the very same time. All of their eyes are lines. They have aggravated lines in their whole faces.

"This is the last straw," Mom says.

Last straw? Everybody hates last straws, and I don't even know what those things are. But I hate them too.

Then Dad says, "Go to your room, Natalie."

And those chokey tears leak out of me. "I'm ... *sniff* ... sorry. All ... *sniff, sniff* ... I wanted to do ... *sniff* ... was a one-of-a-kind wonderful thing!"

I run away to my room.

I think I hear my daddy calling me, "Natalie? Nat?"

I think I hear Mom saying, "Nat? Honey?"

But I am running too fast to stop.

I run all the way to my room because I am done with this one-of-a-kind horrible day.

Chapter 12

Only Nat

When I am in my bedroom, I run to my bed. But there are a hundred gazillion animals on there. I knock them all off of my bed, except for not Steg-O.

And not Percy. Percy is curled up on my pillow.

I climb into my bed upside down because that's how I feel. My head is where my feet should be, and my feet are next to Percy on my pillow. When I'm all the way in, I pull all the covers over my head.

I am upside down in my bed because this was an upside-down, NOT wonderful day. That's what.

I have an alone feeling that makes me sad in my heart. So I peek outside my covers until I see Steg-O. Then I grab Steg-O and bring him in here with me under the covers.

Percy wakes up and crawls under the covers with me and Steg-O. When I pet Percy's head, he purrs like he does for my mom. And that can make me chokey because it's a nice thing.

"Percy and Steg-O," I whisper, kind of chokey, "I am *Lizard Breath*."

This is what Peter called me when he pulled my hair in the grocery store. That's 'cause he heard my mom say "Elizabeth" in the middle of my name when I stuck my gum on the shopping cart. Peter shouted, "You are Elizabeth the Lizard Breath!"

So now I am thinking he was right when he said that mean thing about me. I *am* a lizard breath.

"I will start going by the name of Elizabeth Lizard Breath," I tell Percy and Steg-O, 'cause they are the only ones here under the covers with me.

Only then I remember that there is someone else

in here with Percy and Steg-O and me.

And I know this is a true thing because that someone is in every place, even under covers. And that someone goes by the name of — you guessed it — God. Plus also, Jesus.

So I talk to God because it is very nice of God to be in a place with a lizard breath who can't do anything wonderful. Plus also, God is a better listener than Percy, who is already trying to get out of here.

"I'm sorry," I start off to God.

I always like talking to God and Jesus. Only this time, the pictures and words in my head are getting in my way.

I have one picture in my head of my mom great big in her eyes when she saw the kitchen after I made the purple grape omel-nat. And that picture has words with it. And those words are "Only Natalie."

And those are the same words in my head with a picture of purple not between the lines on the bathroom wall.

Plus those words are coming from my dad when he stared at his stickery church shoes.

And the ants in the plant …

Only Natalie.

"I don't like being Only Natalie," I tell God under the covers.

I can feel God trying to take some of that sad out of my heart. And that works a little.

But there is a whole lot of sad in there.

I hear footsteps outside my room. They get closer and closer.

I stay under the covers with Percy and Steg-O and God. And I keep very quiet.

My door squeaks opens. "Natalie?" Mom says.

I stay under the covers. I don't say anything again.

"Guess Natalie is asleep," Daddy says.

I hear their footsteps stepping right up to my bed.

"She's asleep upside down," Mom says.

I feel the covers pulling back from me. So I squeeze my eyes very tight shut.

"I'll put her right-side up," Daddy says. He picks me up off the bed and turns me around and puts me back with my head on my pillow and my feet where feet are supposed to go. He is a strong daddy.

I still squeeze my eyes shut. Only I peek a little and see my mom pulling my blankets back over me and tucking in my toes like I like it.

"Well," Daddy says, "this is our time to pray with Nat for her nighttime bedtime prayers. What are we going to do about that?"

This is a true thing. We always pray my nighttime bedtime prayers at night when I go to bed.

Mom says, "I guess we could pray Nat's bedtime prayers without Nat."

This makes me a teeny tiny bit sadder in my heart. I love my nighttime bedtime prayers.

"Dear God," Daddy says, "thank you for this wonderful day you've given us. And most of all, thank you for giving us our wonderful daughter, Natalie 24."

"I agree with that!" Mom says. "Our Nat is one of a kind, heavenly Father. Who else could make our lives so full and wonderful?"

Who? I am waiting for the answer to that question.

My heart feels very twitchy.

My eyes can't stay squeezed shut.

I have tears in my head. And they come out now. Only they are not coming from the sad place in my heart. I think they are coming from a happy place in there while I wait for that answer to who makes their lives wonderful.

Then Mommy and Daddy both say this at the same time: "Only Natalie."

I sit very fast up in my bed and unsqueeze my two eyes. "Did you say *I'm* wonderful?" I ask Daddy.

Daddy has a smiley face. "You *are* wonderful, Nat."

I look at my mom. She has a smiley face.

"Did you say *I'm* one of a kind?" I ask her.

"You sure are!" Mommy says. "You, Natalie 24, are a one-of-a-kind wonderful kid."

"Amen!" says my dad.

"Amen!" I say, feeling happy in my heart that I'm getting in on my nighttime bedtime prayers after all.

Mommy and Daddy both kiss me good night.

Plus also, I kiss them back.

When they are all gone and my door is closed, I kiss goodnight to my cat, Percy, and my dinosaur, Steg-O.

Then I yawn really big 'cause one-of-a-kind wonderful days make me sleepy. That's what.

And as I float into that sleepiness, my mind whispers thanks to God for making me, Natalie 24, the one-of-a-kind wonderful thing.

Because it turns out I really do like being ...

Only Natalie.

Check out the other books in the series – available now!

Natalie has big five-year-old dreams for her future. So big, that her heart gets thumpy with excitement. Nat uses her very own words to tell about her hopes, struggles, and adventures. This makes the That's Nat! series perfect for young readers just ready for chapter books.

Book 1: Natalie and the One-of-a-Kind Wonderful Day!
ISBN: 978-0-310-71566-5

Book 2: Natalie Really Very Much Wants to Be a Star
ISBN: 978-0-310-71567-2

Book 3: Natalie: School's First Day of Me
IBSN: 978-0-310-71568-9

Available now at your local bookstore!

Check out the other books in the series – available now!

Book 4: Natalie and the Downside-Up Birthday
ISBN: 978-0-310-71569-6

Book 5: Natalie and the Bestest Friend Race
ISBN: 978-0-310-71570-2

Book 6: Natalie Wants a Puppy, That's What
IBSN: 978-0-310-71571-9

Available now at your local bookstore!

My Little Purse Bible

ISBN: 978-0-310-82266-0

This is an adorable purse-like Bible cover that comes with a complete New Testament edition of the NIrV translation with Psalms and Proverbs. This is available for a limited time and perfect for the Easter Holiday.

Available now at your local bookstore!

Adventure Bible for Early Readers, NIrV
ISBN: 978-0-310-71547-4

Now kids 6-9 can share in the love for God's Word with The Adventure Bible for Early Readers. Based on the bestselling Adventure Bible and written in the New International Reader's Version (NIrV—"The NIV for Kids!"), this Bible is designed especially for early readers who are ready to explore the Bible on their own.

The Adventure Bible for NIrV: Book of Devotions for Early Readers
ISBN: 978-0-310-71448-4

Buckle up, hold tight, and get ready for adventure! The NIrV Adventure Bible Book of Devotions for Early Readers takes kids on the ride of their lives. This yearlong devotional carries young children on a thrilling journey of spiritual growth and discovery.

Available now at your local bookstore!